BLOOD RED ROSES
Lin Anderson

A Prequel to *Driftnet*
with Forensic Scientist Dr Rhona MacLeod

When does desire become obsession?

A hen night in Glasgow leaves the bride-to-be
dead on a toilet floor. Her body is twisted, her
face a mask of terror. Who would kill a girl just
before her wedding? Dr Rhona MacLeod and her
team are called in to find out. As they go
through the evidence, they find themselves in a
world where sex is bought and sold, and more
violent death is lying in wait.

Lin Anderson is a crime novelist and
screenwriter. Her first novel, *Driftnet*, became
a Scottish bestseller in August 2003 and has
since sold to Germany, France and Russia.
Blood Red Roses is a prequel to *Driftnet*.
Lin lives in Edinburgh, with her husband, John.
She has two sons and one daughter.

By the same author

Fiction
Driftnet
Torch

BLOOD RED ROSES

Lin Anderson

SANDSTONE vista 4

The Sandstone Vista Series

Blood Red Roses
First published 2005 in Great Britain by Sandstone Press Ltd
PO Box 5725, Dingwall, Ross-shire, IV15 9WJ, Scotland

The publisher acknowledges the financial support of both the
Highland Council, through the Education, Culture and Sport
Service, and the Literacies Initiative of the Highland
Community Learning and Development Strategy Partnership.

ISBN 0-9546333-5-0

The Sandstone Vista Series of books has
been written and skilfully edited
for the enjoyment of readers with differing levels
of reading skills, from the emergent to the accomplished.

Designed and typeset by Edward Garden Graphic Design,
Dingwall, Ross-shire, Scotland.

Printed and bound by Dingwall Printers Ltd,
Dingwall, Ross-shire, Scotland.

www.sandstonepress.com

Dedicated to Detective Inspector Bill Mitchell

CHAPTER ONE

She smiled and he wanted the smile to be for him.

In his mind he licked the blood red lips, tasting sugary alcopops and lip gloss.

Then the others joined in, cackling and crowing. His face flushed with anger.

'Hey – we're here – come on!'

The doors opened and the hen party spilled onto the underground platform, waving plastic pitchforks, spiked tails swaying, devil horns blinking red. Hanging back, he waited for the five bobbing heads to reach the escalator before he followed.

Three clubs later she was drunk and needing the toilet. He was waiting on the other side of the saloon doors. She turned a glassy surprised eye on him.

'What are you doing here?'

He smiled and handed her a drink.

'Taking a last look before you become a married woman.'

She believed him. They chinked bottles.

'To a long and happy marriage.'

She met his smile. 'To a long and happy marriage.'

He watched her swallow three quarters of the bottle.

'Wow,' she said. 'Now I do need a piss.'

She pushed open the toilet door, her knees already buckling, then fell, hard. The bottle smashed against a sink, exploding in a shower of rainbow glass.

Her heels began to drum the floor; her hands clawed the air. Foamy spittle bubbled out of her lips as they turned blue. Her eyes widened in terror. She tried desperately to draw air into her lungs, her chest heaving.

Now his smile was genuine. Served her right, the bitch.

CHAPTER TWO

Dr Rhona MacLeod looked up as the waiter sat a bottle of chilled white wine and two glasses on the table.

'I didn't order ...' she began.

'Compliments of the band.'

It was after midnight and the crowds were thinning. DI Bill Wilson was still there, arms locked round Margaret his wife of thirty years, swaying to the haunting sounds of the saxophone. He was enjoying the remnants of his fiftieth birthday party. The police could throw a hell of a do when required. Even Bill's boss had managed a five-minute appearance, to drink a glass of champagne, before he went off to dinner with someone more important.

Rhona poured herself a glass of wine. The saxophone drew to the end of its piece, sending shivers down her spine. She wasn't a jazz fan. But tonight had almost changed her mind.

'Hey.' Chrissy, her forensic assistant, appeared at her side, a young man by the hand. 'We're off.' She raised an eyebrow at the wine and glasses.

'From the band,' Rhona told her.

Chrissy ran a practised eye over the men on stage.

'Hope it's the saxophone player.'

It was, but Rhona didn't say.

'See you tomorrow then.'

Rhona smiled back. 'See you.'

Chrissy pranced off, dazed young constable in tow. Rhona secretly wished him luck.

The saxophonist thanked his audience in an Irish accent as though he meant it. He sat the saxophone on its stand, jumped from the stage and came towards her.

'Hi.' His eyes were very blue. 'I'm Sean. Can we talk?'

They talked while the rest of the band packed up. Bill came to say goodbye. He looked happy, his arm round Margaret. Rhona was pleased he'd had a good time. Bill deserved the respect his colleagues paid him. He was a good guy and a good policeman. He complimented Sean on his performance and winked at Rhona.

'Come on,' Margaret pulled him away. 'It's time I took you home, birthday boy.'

Then they were alone apart from the barman, who handed Sean the keys.

'You lock up. I'm off.'

'I own a part share in the club,' Sean explained as the door shut and silence fell.

Rhona wondered how much of this was planned. How many women Sean had seduced with his blue eyes, Irish voice and saxophone. At this moment she didn't care.

'There's a tune I'd like you to hear.'

He stood on stage, eyes closed, caressing the golden instrument. The sound was dark and sensual. Mood music.

'That was great,' she said when he finished. 'What's it called?'

'*For You.*'

She laughed at his cheeky grin. Irish charm. Who could beat it?

They walked towards her flat, side by side, not

touching.

Being alone had always been her choice. She loved her work, her flat, her life. If or when men came it was good but never permanent. She wondered if she would invite him up, already knowing she would. Between them was something inevitable, although probably short-lived.

They didn't speak as they climbed the stairs. She unlocked the door and they stepped inside. He undressed her in the hallway, so slowly she wanted to scream at him to hurry. His tongue flicked her lips until she opened her mouth to him.

Her mobile rang, pulling her from sleep. She reached down, searching for her handbag, suddenly remembering. Sean was stretched out beside her, easy in sleep. She checked herself for regret and found none.

She slipped out of bed and found her bag ringing in the hall.

'Rhona?'

'Bill.'

'Sorry to wake you.'

'What's wrong?'

'I'm at the *Excalibur* pub near the Arches. Female body in the toilets.'

'I'll be there in fifteen minutes.'

She shook Sean awake.

As she pulled on clothes, he told her he would wait for her to come back.

She looked at him, puzzled.

'I make good coffee,' he explained.

She nodded, already thinking about death.

She pulled the front door behind her, knowing he wouldn't be there when she got back. Making love to a forensic scientist might be exciting. Waiting for her to come back from a murder scene was not.

Excalibur had a big sword above the door. Long and hard. Frequented mainly by singles, the symbol promised more than it could deliver.

Bill was waiting in the corridor beyond the saloon doors. He looked at her, bleary eyed.

'Happy birthday,' she said.

He pointed her towards the toilets.

The twisted body was sprawled half in, half out of a cubicle, devil horns blinking red. She wore black lycra, stretched over full breasts. A forked tail lay motionless on the tiles among the broken glass of an alcopop bottle.

'A hen night,' Bill said. 'Her mate found her. They called 999. The paramedic that tried mouth to mouth reported a strange tingling in his lips. He called us.'

Rhona ran a latex-gloved finger over the blue lips then touched her own. The spot she touched tingled then went numb. She picked up a piece of glass and sniffed it.

'What's up?' Bill said.

'Not sure. Could be poison.'

Bill looked surprised. 'I thought it was drugs.'

Rhona took a sample of the small sticky pool of browny-purple liquid.

'I'll collect the glass. If she was poisoned, the bottle was the murder weapon.'

Rhona cleared the face of hair and caught a faint scent of something other than booze and makeup.

'Did she have asthma?'

'Her mates are next door. We'll ask.'

Four devils sat side by side, smeared mascara,

eyes clouded by drink. Three seemed unable to speak. Rhona spoke to the fourth, who said her name was Tracey.

'We were pissed,' she muttered. 'Donna went to the toilet and never came back. I went looking for her. She was jerking and moaning. It was horrible. I got scared and called 999 on my mobile.' She looked at Rhona. 'She's dead, isn't she?'

Rhona nodded.

'We drank the same amount. How come she's dead?' Tears ran black down her cheeks. 'She was getting married tomorrow.'

'We'll need to inform her family.'

'She didn't have one. Only her mates... and Jonny.'

'Jonny?' Rhona said.

'Her fiance.' She spat out the word.

'You didn't like him?' Bill said.

Tracey was defiant. 'He wanted Donna to change. I liked her the way she was.'

'Did Donna take her drink to the toilet with her?' Rhona asked.

Tracey looked puzzled. 'Why would she do that?'

'Was she asthmatic?'

'What?'

'Did she have asthma?'

'Not that I know of.'

'Are any of you asthmatic?'

They shook their heads.

'Fucked up, yes,' Tracey said. 'Asthmatic no.'

Rhona opened her forensic bag and set about taking samples. The girl's body was already showing signs of rigor mortis. The muscle stiffening and the macabre grin suggested poison, probably strychnine. But finding the cause of death was the pathologist's job. Hers was to find traces of the attacker.

There was no evidence of violent or sexual assault, apart from grazed skin from the broken bottle. Rhona sampled the lips and bagged the gloved hands. Then she set about picking up the glass.

The pathologist arrived as she was finishing. Dr Sissons gave her a weary look.

'Drugs or drink?'

Rhona shook her head. 'At a guess, strychnine poisoning.'

Now she had his interest. Poisonings were not the usual manner of violent death in Glasgow on a Friday night.

When Rhona got back to the flat, dawn was streaking the sky with red. Her cat, Chance, ran towards her, looking for food. She smelt coffee, then heard Sean humming. Naked, he smiled as she entered the kitchen.

'Okay?'

She nodded, unsure whether she wanted him there or not.

He tipped a measure of whisky in the coffee and carried it into the bedroom.

'Want to talk?'

'No.'

'Good.'

When he moved against her she forgot the blue lips and twisted limbs. She forgot death and celebrated life.

CHAPTER THREE

Bill was seated in his favourite chair. It looked out of place in the modern office. Old leather, with a girn that could not be oiled into silence, it gave him a place to think.

'Poison,' he shook his head. 'It's like an Agatha Christie novel.'

'Strychnine. She died quickly, if horribly.'

'Jonny, the fiance, is a fireman.'

'A suspect?'

'How many husbands-to-be kill their bride on her hen night?'

'We've had weirder murders.'

Bill shook his head. The world of murder was as strange as it had been when he started in the force thirty years before.

Detective Constable Janice Clarke stuck her head round the door.

'Car's here, sir.'

'Ready?'

Rhona nodded.

Donna Steven's flat was in a block on the lower end of Maryhill Road, minutes from Charing Cross. Bill left the driver with the car to safeguard his tyres.

A team was already there. Three white suits greeted Rhona as she entered from the walkway.

The flat was tiny. A kitchen-living room, a bedroom, cramped hall and bathroom. In the bedroom an ivory wedding dress hung on a wardrobe door. On the dressing table sat a fairytale veil. Rhona fingered the dress material, recognising the smooth feel of expensive silk.

She tried to imagine what Donna had been thinking and feeling the last time she was in this room.

'Civil wedding. A small guest list but no expense spared,' Bill told her.

'What did she do for a living?'

'Worked in a newsagent, Tracey says'.

Rhona glanced again at the wedding frock. 'If she didn't have a family...'

'I take it the dress is expensive?'

'Silk. A couple of thousand I would say.'

'Bloody hell!'

Bill had a teenage daughter and a son. Chances were he would be counting the cost shortly himself.

'So where was the money coming from?' Bill said.

'The husband-to-be?'

'The guy's in shock. I'll interview him later.'

'Can I take a look at the room... by myself?'

Bill nodded. 'Be my guest.'

Rhona's mentor in the early days had been Dr Fields, or Eagle-eye as he was fondly known. He did everything. Medical, fibres, fingerprints, all the branches. He taught her how to get results from what was called reticent evidence. Evidence not willing to give up its secrets. One thing more he'd taught her. Forensics can help, but only if you know what to look for. To know that, you have to get to know the victim.

The wedding dress dominated the room. Below it was a pair of matching silk shoes. A wave of emotion swept over Rhona. Donna wanted to get married. Did someone poison her to stop that happening?

Beside the shoes sat a small wastepaper basket. Below a couple of makeup tissues was a single red rose, wilting from lack of water.

Rhona carefully removed it and slipped it in a forensic bag.

Fifteen minutes later Bill was at the door. 'Find anything?'

'Small spots of blood on the bed cover. And some hair samples from the pillow that don't look like Donna's.'

She showed him the rose. 'And this.'

Bill sniffed. 'Shop roses don't usually have a scent.'

'Is Jonny a gardener?'

'He lives in a flat above the fire station. Anyway, garden roses don't flower in November, do they?'

Bill dropped her off at the forensic lab, promising to get in touch after he'd interviewed Jonny Simpson.

Rhona loved the view from her laboratory window, even now in November. She looked down on Kelvingrove Park, the Art Gallery and

Museum in the distance. The museum had been her favourite haunt both as a child with her father and later as a student studying at Glasgow University.

Chrissy appeared from the back lab and gave Rhona a look.

'What?' Rhona played the innocent.

'Was it the saxophonist?'

Rhona laughed.

'I knew it. And?'

'And what?' said Rhona, putting on her lab coat.

Chrissy pulled a face. 'You're not going to tell me, are you?'

Rhona shook her head.

'Must have been good.'

'Chrissy,' Rhona warned.

'Okay, okay.' Chrissy took the hint.

Rhona began unpacking her forensic bag.

'The bride in the toilet?'

'I went to her flat with Bill. There was a very expensive wedding dress hanging in the bedroom...'

'Poor cow... '

'And this...'

Rhona showed Chrissy the rose.

'Maybe she had another admirer. One that Jonny didn't know about,' Chrissy suggested.

'Or one he found out about...'

CHAPTER FOUR

Jonny Simpson sat with his head in his hands.

DI Wilson had seen all kinds of grief in thirty years as a policeman. It always left its mark. And you had to be careful. Genuine grief didn't always look the way you thought it should.

'Okay Mr Simpson. Tell me about the last time you saw Donna.'

Jonny lifted a white face.

'I haven't seen Donna since Wednesday night. I've been on call.'

'Did you speak to her?'

'We sent texts.'

'And what did she say in these texts?'

Jonny's face flushed. 'Just private stuff.'

Bill was familiar with the world of text messaging, due to his two teenage children. Text was like email. You could write things you might not say.

'Tracey says Donna didn't have a family.'

Jonny's face clouded over. 'Donna was brought up in a children's home. She only had me.'

'Where did you two meet?'

Jonny hesitated for a second or two. 'In the newsagent where she works. I get my paper there.'

'Getting married is an expensive business,' Bill said.

Jonny glared at him. 'If you mean the dress, Donna's been saving for it since she was sixteen. I don't care about all that, but it was important to her.'

Bill decided to get to the point.

'Did you give Donna a rose?'

'What?'

'We found a red rose in the wastepaper bin in her bedroom.'

Jonny tried to mask the quick look of jealousy that flashed across his face.

'I don't remember.'

'Try.'

'These folk come round the pubs, trying to sell you a rose. Donna was soft. She made me buy them sometimes.'

It was a good answer. Bill almost believed him.

'Why are you talking to me anyway? Why aren't you out there catching the bastard that killed Donna?'

'We'd like you to provide a DNA sample, Mr Simpson.'

'You think I killed her?'

'We need to eliminate you from our enquiry.'

Jonny took a look at Bill's calm face and relaxed.

'I'll do whatever it takes to catch him.'

'Donna had an admirer,' Bill told Rhona later. 'Or Jonny suspects she did.'

'Someone who might give her a rose?'

'Remember the murderer we got because he shared an orange with his victim?'

'Just what I was thinking,' Rhona said. 'The drops of blood on the coverlet weren't Donna's.'

'What about Jonny?'

'We're checking. We've also identified three types of head hair from the pillow. One is Donna's. The other two are likely to be men. We have roots so a DNA analysis is possible. We'll check them against Jonny. Chrissy's taking a look at the sheets for semen.'

'You think Donna was playing away?'

'Could be. And there were traces of salbutomal on her hair.'

'So someone asthmatic was close to her before she died?'

Rhona considered this. It wasn't uncommon for rapists to take a shot of an inhaler before making their move on a victim. They were so worked up that an asthma attack could be on the cards.

'There was no evidence of sexual assault,' Bill reminded her.

'Maybe watching Donna die was thrill enough.'

A smiling Chrissy left the lab at six to meet PC Williams, the young constable she had met the evening before. Rhona stayed on to work on the Bacardi Coke bottle. On arrival that morning, she'd filled an empty bottle with a mixture of plaster of Paris, stuck a thin wooden rod down the neck and set it to harden.

Now, using the rod as a handle, she took a small hammer and gently tapped the side of the bottle until it cracked in several places. Then she held it over the waste bin and gave the bottle three short sharp knocks. The glass fell away in dozens of shards.

Now she had a plastic replica of the bottle, she could start putting the murder weapon together again. Chrissy had laughed when Rhona produced the Bacardi Coke bottle that morning. She laughed even harder when she heard Rhona's plan.

'No chance,' had been Chrissy's expert opinion.

Rhona suspected Chrissy was right, but she had to give it a try.

She arranged all the pieces she'd picked up on a tray. She would start the long slow process of fitting the jigsaw together tomorrow.

Outside, Rhona shivered in the raw night air. She hadn't brought the car. She could have tried for a taxi but decided to walk. Walking helped her think.

Street lights threw pools of yellow on grey puddles. The rain had dwindled to a faint mist that masked sound. Cars swished past throwing water in her path. Rhona strode on too absorbed to notice. In her head she was replaying the scene that had ended in Donna's death.

Donna had been given a Bacardi Coke outside the ladies toilet. There were no signs of force so Donna took the drink willingly. But that didn't mean she knew her murderer. Rhona hoped she did. If they were dealing with a psycho who had no link with the victim, it would be even more difficult to find him.

Bill had questioned Donna's mates. They insisted Donna was seeing no one but Jonny. They also said they had seen nobody they knew on the night of the hen party. Only Tracey seemed wary. Wary and scared, according to Bill.

CHAPTER FIVE

'Where the fuck is she?'

Tracey couldn't tell him the truth. 'She's not well.'

Belcher's fat sweaty face grew redder.

'Tell her she's fired if she doesn't turn up tomorrow night.'

He shoved a rose at Tracey. 'You do it. Room five and make it good.'

The green baize walls and heavily carpeted hallway smothered all sound. Tracey passed four doors and stood outside number five, waiting for the double vodka to swim through her blood stream.

There were four of them. Spiked hair, designer stubble, muscled bodies under patterned short-sleeved shirts. A stag night maybe? Or just guys who liked getting off on girls like her.

'Hi Rose. Come on in.'

They were seated round a circular table, three champagne bottles in the middle. One of them handed her a full glass and watched her drink it in a oner.

The music came on. She started on the blonde one with the pale eyes because he looked harmless. She unbuttoned his shirt and with the rose in her mouth traced his smooth chest, lower and lower until she reached his hardening crotch.

The others yelled in delight.

Jonny came in at midnight and took a seat at the bar. Tracey had finished her stint with the four guys and badly needed a drink. She didn't see Jonny until it was too late.

He grabbed her arm and forced her onto the stool beside him. His face was a mask of hate.

'She was still doing this, wasn't she? That's how she was paying for the fucking dress.'

Tracey didn't answer.

'It's your fault she's dead. You and the rest of her fucking friends.'

He was right. She had told Donna to stay on at the club. The money was good. She could buy the dress she wanted. She'd persuaded Donna that what Jonny didn't know couldn't hurt him.

'Some bastard gave her a rose. I want to know who it was.'

Tracey recoiled as though she'd been punched. 'What?'

'The police found a red rose at the flat. They think I gave it to her, but I didn't, did I, Tracey?'

Tracey couldn't speak. She was thinking about the dance she'd just performed. Rose's dance.

When Jonny left, she headed for the toilet. She reached the cubicle just in time. A mix of vodka and champagne hit the pan. She pressed her face against the cool toilet seat, her body shaking.

Jonny had made her promise not to tell the police about Donna's job here and the guy who kept coming back again and again to see her dance as Rose. He also made her promise to carry on doing what Belcher wanted.

'They said you're good,' Belcher had told her when she'd finished with the four guys. 'Very satisfying.' He said the words like he had a hard-on himself. 'You're the new Rose.' He poked a fat finger in her face. 'And you can tell Donna that from me.'

She wanted to shout at him. 'Donna's dead you stupid bastard. She's dead!'

But she had said nothing, her stomach tight with fear.

'The sicko will come back,' Jonny's eyes had glinted revenge as he left. 'He'll be looking for another Rose. And I'll be waiting for him.'

CHAPTER SIX

Mrs Harper opened her front door as Rhona came up the stairs. In her arms were a dozen red roses.

'These were delivered this afternoon,' she told Rhona with a wide smile.

Her neighbour had set her sights on seeing Rhona 'settled down' as she put it, and took a keen interest in her love life... when there was any.

Rhona waited until she was inside the flat before she looked at the card. It simply said 'For you'.

The rush of pleasure the words brought surprised her. She hadn't thought about Sean all day. She never mixed work and pleasure.

While the bath filled, she fed Chance and poured herself a glass of wine. Her kitchen window looked down on the gardens of a convent.

In daylight it offered a tranquil scene. At night, soft light lit up a statue of the Virgin Mary that stood in the centre of the lawn.

The tolling of the convent bell for prayers was part of her life. Rhona loved its certainty, although for her there was no certainty in life, except death.

She slipped low in the water, enjoying the heat on her skin. Sex with Sean had been good. Better than good. Thinking about it now brought a second rush of pleasure.

The question was, did she want to get involved? Great sex was one thing. A proper relationship was another.

The buzzer went at midnight. Rhona knew it was Sean before she answered.

When she let him in, he stood uncertain in the hall.

'I woke you,' he said taking in the dressing gown.

'No,' she answered. 'I was reading.'

She was greedy for him but still she didn't move.

'Rhona...'

Then she was in his arms, her mouth on his.

Her body screaming for him.

Later they lay in the dark, his heart beating gently against her cheek.

'We're good at this.' His voice was light.

He was like her, she thought. Alone but not lonely. Self-contained. Maybe it would work?

'We could give it a try?' He echoed her own thoughts.

Rhona touched his nipple and felt it harden.

CHAPTER SEVEN

Bill Wilson had interviewed the girlfriends again and got nowhere. They were adamant they had seen no-one they recognised on the hen night. Only when he asked them how they knew Donna, did they stumble. The stories they told him didn't ring true. Especially Tracey's.

She sat in front of him now, her eyes bloodshot, her brow slick with sweat. She was nursing a hangover or dealing with a drug habit or she was shit scared. Bill suspected the latter.

'There's something you're not telling me, Tracey.' He hated seeing the lassie in this state and it sounded in his voice.

She didn't look at him, her hands plucking at the denim mini skirt. But he sensed her weakening.

'We met at work... at a club called... *Eden*.'

He'd heard of it. He waited for her to go on.

'Lap-dancing. Donna performed as Rose.'

'Performed?'

'She used a rose in the routine.'

He didn't ask her to explain the routine. He had a pretty good idea already.

'There was a guy. Came almost every night for weeks.'

'You saw him?'

'No. Rose... Donna told me about him though.'

'What did she tell you?

'He always brought his own rose. Made her dig the thorns into him.'

Bill felt the surge of excitement that came with the first breakthrough. Rhona had been right. The rose was important. Maybe even a direct link with the murderer.

'Did Donna say what he looked like?'

She shook her head. 'He was young. Worked out. That's all.'

'Thank you Tracey.'

She met his eyes. Hers were tearful. He thought of his own teenage daughter, as safe as he could keep her. It made Bill want to weep too.

Mr Belcher wasn't impressed to see Rhona and DI Wilson enter his club. He was even less impressed when they said they wanted to forensically examine the private room Rose danced in.

'Rose is gone. I sacked her.'

'Rose's real name was Donna Stevens,' Bill told him. 'And Donna is dead, Mr Belcher. She was murdered.'

Belcher's face was a mix of emotions and sympathy wasn't one of them.

'What has that got to do with my club?'

'We think her murderer met her here.'

Belcher gave Bill a sharp look. 'You don't know that...'

'We have trace material,' Rhona interrupted. 'If we find a match in the room...'

'I won't have my club involved in this.'

Bill ignored the bluster. 'I want a list of all your regulars and their contact details.'

Belcher was growing paler by the minute. 'Our customers are mostly casual.'

He was lying. It was written in big letters across his face. Rhona suspected there would be names on that list that didn't want to see the light of day. Bill didn't care.

'And include a list of all credit card payments.'

Belcher showed them to room five, then scuttled off to call his lawyer.

'I'll manage here,' Rhona told Bill.

'You're sure?'

'Give me an hour.'

The room was too warm and smelt of perfume and stale cigarette smoke. It didn't look clean either, which suited Rhona fine. She locked the door and went on to sample every inch of the hideous green carpet.

The roses for the performance were usually supplied by the management. But one customer brought his own. A crushed petal from that rose could be a link to Donna's flat.

CHAPTER EIGHT

She needed the money. That's what Tracey kept reminding herself. She had told the police. She'd done all she could.

Belcher had insisted she use Donna's area of the dressing room as though it was a move up in the world. In the mirror her face was a mask of glossed lips and blackened eyes. Tracey rubbed the rose-scented oil into her skin and put on the red thong and bra.

Room seven had become the Rose room for tonight, Belcher told her. He did not explain why. Her first customer was waiting.

It was the blonde guy from the foursome. He looked sheepish, scared even. She remembered his embarrassment. His cock had shrivelled when she'd unzipped him.

'I wanted to apologise for my mates,' he began.

'You could have done that without paying.'

His eyes ran over her, fastening on her breasts.

'If you just like looking...'

He nodded.

She reached round and unhooked the bra. Her breasts fell, oiled and heavy.

Two glasses of chilled champagne stood on the table. He handed her one. She touched her nipple and made it harden, watching his reaction. At least he only wanted to look.

The heavily carpeted corridor was deserted but Rhona sensed people behind the row of closed doors.

Belcher came hurrying over as she re-entered the bar. His attempt at a smile made him look like a gargoyle in the purple light. His lawyer must have told him to co-operate ... up to a point.

'You've finished? Good.'

'Is Tracey here?'

The smile disappeared. He made a show of checking the reservation book.

'I'm afraid Tracey's dancing at the moment.'

Rhona took a seat at the bar.

'I'll wait.'

His eyes darted about. He was working out whether that would put the punters off.

'If you'd like to wait in my office?'

'Here's fine.'

Belcher gave up and nodded at the barman who slid the drinks list across the counter. Rhona glanced at the prices. It wasn't only private dance routines that cost the earth in here.

The smile was pasted back on Belcher's face.

'On the house of course.'

Rhona ordered a mineral water and took a good look round. The clients were all male except for herself and a girl wrapped round a pole. Rhona recognised the girl as one of the devils from the hen party. Her eyes were glazed, her movements were fluid. The pole was holding her up.

Young men circled the stage, faces eager and aroused. Round the walls the men who didn't fancy being seen were in dark booths. Now and again Belcher appeared and led a group through the green door for their private session.

By the time Bill came back, Rhona had been chatted up twice. Once by a guy old enough to be her father. The second time by a guy young enough to be her son. She was glad to see Bill.

'How'd it go?' he said.

'Fine. I asked to speak to Tracey.'

'And?'

'She's dancing.'

Belcher was showing in the next group. Bill stepped in front of him.

'Get Tracey in here now.'

Belcher's mouth opened and shut a few times.

'I'll send her out.'

When he re-appeared he was alone, an irritated look on his face.

'Tracey's gone.'

'If this is a wind up...'

Belcher shook his head. 'She was in seven, the Rose room for tonight. With a single guy. The room's empty and she's not in the dressing area.'

Rhona pushed past him, a sick feeling in her stomach.

The door to seven stood open. An oily scent of roses hit her at the entrance. That and the musky smell of sex.

CHAPTER NINE

One girl dead and another girl missing. Rhona didn't want to think that something bad had happened to Tracey.

If she was as scared as Tracey, she would probably run. Which is what she hoped Tracey had done.

Bill extracted Tracey's address from the pole dancer and they drove round there. Neither of them expected to find Tracey at home.

The basement bedsit, complete with barred windows, was near the Kelvin Hall. The door was opened by a short balding man in his fifties. He took a long look at Bill's ID card before he let them in.

Tracey had gone out a couple of hours ago, he told them. She hadn't come back. Rhona didn't like the man, but thought he was probably telling the truth.

Tracey's room was untidy and smelt musty. The wardrobe and drawers were stacked with clothes. If Tracey had run, she hadn't taken much with her.

Bill went out to the car to call the station while Rhona took a closer look.

A half-empty bottle of vodka sat on the dressing table beside the picture of a small boy of about three on a swing. He was so like Tracey, he had to be her son. The child obviously didn't live here. Could Tracey have gone to wherever he was?

Rhona heard Bill in the hall.

'I've put out a call on Tracey.'

Rhona handed him the photo.

'Tracey had a kid?'

'Looks like it. I think you should ask for a forensic team to go over this room too.'

'Tricky. This isn't even a missing person case yet.'

'Okay. I'll do it myself, unofficially for the moment.' She didn't add until we find a body. By the look on Bill's face, he was thinking the same thing.

It was dark as they drove back to the lab. Bill's

wife called him on the way, reminding him to come home and eat. For a moment, Rhona wished someone was waiting at home for her.

The lab was deserted. Everyone including Chrissy had left. Rhona set to work, enjoying the silence.

The pathologist had confirmed strychnine had been used to kill Donna. The large dose she was given killed her quickly, probably because of a weak heart. Otherwise Donna's agony might have lasted even longer.

A rose expert had promised to get back to Rhona on the breed of rose found in Donna's flat. Something special could prove easier to track down.

An hour later she had what she was looking for. Minute traces of blood on three of the rose's thorns. If the guy who liked his sex rough was Donna's murderer, they had his blueprint.

.

CHAPTER TEN

Jonny Simpson wasn't due back at work for a week. His honeymoon week, the supervisor reminded Bill.

Bill thanked him and put the phone down.

Tracey's feelings about Jonny Simpson had never been fully explained. And now Bill couldn't ask her. Nine times out of ten the murderer was someone the victim knew. Men regularly killed their wives and their girlfriends. Jonny had lied about the rose. He was jealous of someone or something.

As far as Bill was concerned there were two men in the frame for the murder. Jonny and the mystery guy who visited Donna regularly at the club.

Rhona had a DNA sample from blood on the rose. It would prove whether Jonny had handled the rose but it wouldn't prove he killed Donna.

Bill didn't like to think about the third scenario. That the murderer had chosen Donna at random. With no other motive than the desire to kill.

Jonny's room above the fire station was empty. His mates hadn't seen him since the news about Donna. His best man, Alistair Banks, also a fireman, had no idea where Jonny was.

'He said he needed to get away for a couple of days. Sort his head out. He was devastated about Donna.'

'Did Jonny say anything about Donna seeing someone else?'

Banks looked genuinely surprised.

'No way. You should have seen them together. Donna loved him.'

'And Jonny?'

'Donna was Jonny's girl. He wouldn't have let... '

Bill waited.

'It wouldn't have happened.'

'Donna had a regular spot at the *Eden* club as a lap dancer.' Bill watched the face closely. 'Did Jonny know that?'

A lot of emotions played on Banks' face. Then he decided to come clean.

'Jonny met Donna there. We went in a crowd from the fire station. When they started a relationship, Donna stopped dancing. That's what he told me.'

'Jonny believed she'd stopped?'

Banks nodded.

But Donna hadn't stopped dancing. Was that enough reason for Jonny to kill her? Bill winced at the thought. But he couldn't ignore the fact that Jonny and Tracey had disappeared at about the same time. And that conjured up all sorts of ideas. Most of them bad.

Had Jonny killed his bride-to-be in a fit of rage and Tracey suspected him? If so, Jonny would have to remove Tracey to stop her talking.

Bill had been a policeman for a long time. Some said he had too soft a heart to become a Chief Inspector. He didn't sook up to the right people. He fell out with his superiors too often. He was a free spirit. A loose cannon. Bill didn't care what they said about him. All he cared about was finding out the truth. That's why he and Rhona got along. She was a scientist. But she had a heart. A big one, though she tried not to show it too often. Rhona took every case to heart. Every death. The only way she could help the victim was to solve the case. She was determined about that. It took up all her time and denied her a personal life. Bill wondered for a moment about the saxophone player she'd met at his birthday party. Had it lasted? He secretly wanted Dr Rhona MacLeod to have what he had. Someone to love her. A life outside murder and mayhem. A family.

A family is what neither Donna nor the missing Tracey seemed to have, despite the fact that Tracey was a mother.

DC Clarke had come up with details of Tracey's child. The boy was three. He had been born when Tracey was fifteen. Tracey had refused to have him adopted and he was now in long-term fostering. If she had a photo of the boy, it was likely she was in touch with the foster family. DC Clarke was checking their address with the social work department.

By seven o'clock Rhona had the name of the rose. He could hear her excitement over the phone.

'A new rose. Came on the market summer

2004. Bred from a fragrant garden rose and a cut rose for vase display. Lasts well and smells nice.'

'Well done,' he said and meant it.

'I had help.'

'So where does that get us?'

'The roses are only sold by Marks and Spencer.'

'He didn't grow it?'

'Which explains why it was blooming in November.'

Bill's heart sank. How many people bought roses from Marks and Spencer?

Rhona came in. 'Try the nearest outlets to the club and Donna's flat. If the guy was in the habit of buying them, the shop might remember him.'

'We'll give it a go.'

'No sign of Tracey?'

Bill grunted. 'No. And Jonny's disappeared now too.'

CHAPTER ELEVEN

Rhona went past the jazz club on her way home.

Outside, she read and re-read the advert for the weekly jazz sessions Sean played in, refusing to admit that his name on the billboard was important to her.

It was dark inside. She stumbled down the stairs following the sound of his saxophone. He was practising and his quiet notes matched the beat of her heart.

The same guy was behind the bar, stacking. When he saw her, he melted into the background.

Sean stood alone on stage, lit by a single light, his eyes closed. He was improvising *For You*. He played the tune through simply, then each note took on a partner, became a trio, then a complex variation.

Sean caught sight of her and stopped.

Rhona thought for a moment she had made a mistake. Was she wrong about the situation between them? She hated the effect the thought had on her. Then his face lit up.

'Rhona.'

'I was passing,' she lied.

'I'm glad.'

The barman brought coffee. They sat in the shadow of a booth, opposite one another, and drank it. Sean appeared calm. Rhona was nervous, a feeling she didn't like.

He broke the silence. 'I'm playing tonight. Will you come?'

'I'm not a big jazz fan.'

He was three feet from her, yet she could smell the scent of his skin.

'It takes time to appreciate jazz.'

They were talking but the words meant nothing. Only the physical closeness of their bodies.

'I don't start here for a couple of hours. Have you eaten?'

He took her silence as a no and stood up.

'Let's go,' he said.

Bill phoned in the middle of the meal. Rhona

knew by his voice it was something bad.

'Tracey?'

'The council came to remove a skip from a back alley close to *Eden*. Tracey's body was inside. It looks much like the last one.'

Rhona swore under her breath.

Sean was silent, watching her face.

'I'm on my way.'

She flicked the mobile shut.

'I have to go. When do you finish at the jazz club?'

'Midnight,' he said. 'I'll come round.' It wasn't a question.

Rhona didn't argue because it was what she wanted too.

The twisted body had been removed from the skip and laid in the incident tent. Tracey was almost unrecognisable. Broken masonry sliding down a shute from the roof had beaten and bloodied her. But the typical grin of the strychnine victim was there.

A wave of emotion hit Rhona. Twenty-four hours ago Tracey had been alive. They had known she was scared of something or someone, and they hadn't saved her from this horrible death.

Bill Wilson looked the way she felt.

'Did no one look in the skip before they dropped the stuff down the shute?' Rhona asked in disbelief.

'She was under rubbish. They didn't see her.'

'How the hell did he get her in there?'

If Donna was alive at the time, her limbs would have been jerking all over the place. If she was dead, she would have been a dead weight.

'Maybe he had help?'

Bill was right. There could be more than one of them.

'Someone could be helping him clear up the mess,' she said. 'Someone who has a lot to lose if we find the murderer.'

'I've got a list of *Eden*'s regular customers from Belcher. DC Clarke's going through them now.'

'The important clients won't be on that list.'

Bill made a growling noise in his throat. 'Then I'll find a way to shut the place down.'

When Bill left the tent, Rhona stepped into her white suit. She slipped on the mask and gloves and began her forensic examination of Tracey's body.

CHAPTER TWELVE

They picked up Jonny Simpson at eleven o'clock.
He had turned up at Tracey's flat, shouting the
odds. The landlord didn't like his attitude and
called the police.

Jonny looked rough. Stubble and sleepless
eyes. The haunted look could be fear he was
about to be charged... or sheer misery. Bill wasn't
sure which. Too many roads led to Jonny,
especially now the barman at *Eden* had told them
he had been in there threatening Tracey the night
before she died.

Bill nodded at DC Clarke to start the tape
rolling. He said the necessary details into the
mike then turned to Jonny.

'Why did you want to speak to Tracey?'

Jonny looked up defiantly, but said nothing.

'A barman at *Eden* reported that you were seen

threatening her.'

Jonny's expression didn't change. 'Fuck off.'

'I repeat. Did you threaten Tracey Nickell?'

Jonny examined his hands.

Bill pushed a set of crime scene photos across the desk. He hadn't told Jonny that Tracey was dead... yet. He wanted to see his reaction when he found out (if he didn't know already).

Jonny concentrated on his hands. They were grimy. Bill wondered if he'd been sleeping rough since Donna's death.

Human psychology said that Jonny would look at the photos eventually. He wouldn't be able to help himself. Jonny's head was down but the eyes were swivelling.

Bill spread the photos apart. The mangled remains of Tracey were now clearly visible.

Jonny's body tensed. He turned slightly and took in the photo nearest him. He swallowed. His knuckles shone white with pressure.

'Oh God.'

He covered his face with his hands, his body heaving silent sobs.

Bill pressed the stop button.

'Get Jonny a cup of tea. Make it strong and sweet.'

DC Clarke left.

'You're good Jonny. I'll give you that. Proper little actor... for a soap. But I know you did that,' he stabbed the photo with his forefinger. 'You killed Donna because she was sleeping with someone else, probably for money. Then you killed Tracey because she suspected it was you.'

Jonny jerked his head like a child defiantly saying no.

Janice came in with the tea. Bill took out a small hip flask and tipped in some whisky then pushed it in front of Jonny.

'Drink!'

Jonny lifted the mug, his hand shaking, and gulped at the hot tea.

The words came rushing out.

'I found out Donna was still working at the club, but not until after she died. I went round. I was mad at Tracey because I knew she was in on it. I made her promise to do what Belcher said. Go on acting the whore with the rose. I thought the sicko would come back and I'd get him myself.'

'Then it's your fault Tracey's dead.'

Beside Bill, DC Clarke made a small

disapproving sound.

'This isn't recording sir.'

'It doesn't matter. Jonny's just leaving.'

A look of surprise crossed Jonny's face.

'Go home. Get some sleep,' Bill grabbed the photos and stood up. 'Be back here at eleven tomorrow morning.'

'Thanks.'

'See Mr Simpson out, DC Clarke.'

Bill watched the pair leave the room. He couldn't charge Jonny until he had some evidence that he had been at the murder scene, both murder scenes. And he had to depend on Dr MacLeod for that.

CHAPTER THIRTEEN

Sean wasn't going to show. Rhona tried the mobile number he'd given her but got only the message service. She was angry with herself. She should never have gone to the club. It looked like she was chasing him.

It was after one o'clock, plenty of time to get from the jazz club to here, she told herself one more time. If he arrived now she wouldn't let him in. Better than that she wouldn't be here at all.

She pulled on a short black dress and high heels and grabbed her jacket. Outside it was cold with a clear sky. She walked briskly towards the main road and waved down the first taxi that passed.

'Where to, luv?'

'*Eden.*'

'*Eden*?' he repeated.

'The lap dancing club,' she confirmed.

'Okay.' The driver gave her a look that spoke volumes, but didn't argue.

The city centre was empty except for the usual prostitute on every corner. Above *Eden* a red light blinked on and off illuminating a lap dancer.

'Do you want me to wait for you?'

He obviously thought she had come here to find a wayward boyfriend or husband.

'No, thanks.'

Rhona handed him his fare.

He slipped her a card with her change. 'In case you want a quick exit.'

Rhona waited until he drove off, then skirted the building and entered the back lane. The incident tent was down. The skip had been removed. A couple were fucking against the wall. The guy looked round when Rhona appeared, then went briskly on with what he was doing. The girl gave Rhona a bored look over his shoulder.

The fire doors were wedged open a foot. Rhona slipped inside. The distant sound of dance music beat like a rapid heart in the green corridor.

The women's toilet was empty except for one locked cubicle. Rhona used the mirror to paint on a face and do her hair. Looking at the result, she was satisfied Belcher wouldn't recognise her, if she kept her distance.

The main room was heaving. She pushed her way through the crowds to the bar. The barman wasn't the one from her previous visit. She arranged herself on the stool while he gave her the once over.

'What can I do you for?'

She gave him a friendly smile. 'Looking for a bar job. Who do I speak to?'

He thought for a minute.

'Boss is busy. Important customers,' he rubbed his fingers together to emphasis money. 'Keep an eye on the door right of the stage. That's his office.' He pushed her over a drink. 'Fat guy with a red face. Belcher's the name. And a wee warning. He likes to handle the goods before he hires.'

Rhona took her drink to an empty booth close to the office door. She didn't get to stay alone for long. A guy watched her slide into the seat and immediately came over.

'Can I join you?'

She looked him up and down. 'I'm waiting for

someone.'

His face darkened. 'Who? The invisible fucking man?'

She glanced pointedly at the closed door. 'The boss.'

He muttered something obscene under his breath and went back to join the crowd round the pole dancer.

When Belcher emerged, he had three middle-aged men with him. Rhona recognised one face. From where she wasn't sure. Then it hit her. The guy was something to do with football.

She stared at her drink as Belcher passed. The three guys were set on a private showing. When they disappeared through the baize door, Rhona took her chance.

CHAPTER FOURTEEN

Once inside, she shut the office door and locked it.

It was a large room. In the centre stood a massive oak desk like something out of a Hollywood mafia movie. Belcher, she realised, had ideas above his station. The scent of expensive aftershave and cigar smoke hung in the air. On the left hand wall was a painting hinged back to reveal a two-foot-square screen. Something Bill hadn't found in his search of the premises.

On the screen was a clear image of a room in the green corridor. The room was lit by a flashing red light. A young woman stood open-legged above one of the three men Rhona had seen follow Belcher. There was no sound, but Rhona sensed the beat of the music the girl moved to.

The girl lowered herself, pressing her crotch against the man's face. Then the image changed. Another room, another girl, another dance.

Rhona stood, her heart thumping. Belcher, a voyeur, watched everything from here. Which meant he probably knew who Donna's regular visitor in the 'Rose' room had been.

Before she left she tried a quick look inside the desk. Only the top drawer was unlocked. In it was an open packet of condoms and an inhaler.

Rhona stared, the full impact of the discovery hitting her like a sledgehammer. She had Belcher marked as a voyeur, a sleazy creep who exploited young girls. But a murderer?

She left the inhaler where it was and shut the drawer. She took a quick glance round before she emerged from Belcher's office.

The barman called to her as she walked casually past.

'Any luck?'

She shook her head. 'Too busy with his important guests.'

'Leave your name and contact number,' he said. 'I'll tell him.'

She wrote a made-up name and number on the pad.

'I finish at two thirty,' he offered.

She smiled an apology. 'Some other time.'

'Your loss,' he called after her, as she made for the Ladies.

This time the toilets were empty. She dialled the number the taxi driver had given her. She must have sounded rattled because he said, 'I'll be there in five minutes.'

She waited for three minutes then walked purposefully out. The doorman gave her a look but said nothing. One of the three middle-aged men was getting into a fancy black car. She found a pen in her bag and wrote down the number. Maybe Bill could use it to find out who Belcher's important guests were. As for Belcher...

The taxi arrived and she climbed gratefully in.

'Didn't find him then?'

'What?... no,' she shrugged.

'Where to now?'

She gave him the address of the jazz club. 'I need a couple of minutes there, then home.'

'He's a jazz lover then?'

Rhona didn't answer.

The club was still open, the sound of music and voices drifting out. She hesitated at the top of the stairs, recognising the notes of his saxophone. Sean was still performing. That's why he hadn't come.

She turned and climbed in the taxi.

'Change your mind?'

'Yes.'

She gave him her address and leaned back, feeling foolish and relieved at the same time.

CHAPTER FIFTEEN

The flat was cold. The heating had gone off by now. Rhona put on a warm dressing gown and thick pair of socks and lit the gas fire in the sitting room. When she sat on the sofa, Chance jumped up and joined her, keen to enjoy the warmth of the flames.

There was no point trying to contact Bill until morning. Belcher didn't look as though he was going anywhere.

The cat's purring soothed her. This was why she didn't like relationships. The worry. The uncertainty. Both made sex more exciting but screwed up your emotions... if you let them.

Sean must not be allowed to interfere with her work or her life. He would come and go, as she pleased. When, or if he arrived tonight, then she would decide.

The buzzer wrecked this decision. She pressed the entry button without answering and left the door off the latch. It took seconds for him to climb the stairs. Waiting in the sitting room, she heard the door open and close.

Then there was silence. She wondered if he had gone straight into the bedroom. The thought both unnerved and excited her.

Then instinct told her she had made a mistake. It was not Sean who had entered her flat. It was someone else. Someone she had let in.

Chance jumped to the floor, tail upright, tip flicking from side to side. He made a weird sound, almost a whine, as the door opened. Rhona stood near the fireplace with nowhere to go, her body tensed, ready for flight.

A man she recognised as Jonny Simpson stood framed in the hall light. His stance reminded her of his fireman role, minus the uniform. He was determined and desperate at the same time.

Murderers, she knew, often looked like that before they killed. Hell bent, obsessed, so desperate for that rush of pleasure, nothing would stop them.

He muttered 'the bitch, the bastard' under his

breath. She thought the words were directed at her, then realised he was abusing some picture inside his head. He was drunk or high or mad on grief.

'Jonny?'

His eyes tried to focus. Seeing her he suddenly launched himself forward.

In seconds he had one arm about her, the other wrenched her dressing-gown from her shoulders. It dropped and she was left naked. He grabbed a breast and squeezed so hard her voice became a squeal of pain.

'Jonny. No!'

He met her eyes and let go.

'She fucking kept doing it. I loved her. I told her not to.' He sank on the couch, searching for answers in the flames of the fire.

Rhona fastened the dressing gown tightly round her. Her mobile was in her handbag in the bedroom. The main phone was in the hall. She judged the distance to the door, the path that skirted Jonny.

He was weeping now. Great gulps that wracked his body. He looked up at her.

'I couldn't take it, her working in that place. I

made her promise. But she wanted that fucking dress...'

'I'm going to make us some coffee, Jonny.'

He nodded like a child listening to its mother.

She stood by the kettle, forcing her body to stop shaking. How the hell had he turned up here? She had never met him, only seen his photo and tested his DNA. He must have seen her with Bill somewhere. Then she knew. Jonny must have been at *Eden* tonight. He'd followed her from there.

She spooned coffee into two mugs. She would find a chance to call the police. Meanwhile she would feed him coffee and get him to talk. Instinct told her Jonny hadn't killed Donna. But if he had been watching the club, he might know something that would help find the murderer.

The cat's screech sent her running through. The acrid smell of smoke met her in the hall. Jonny's arm was already well ablaze, the flames licking across his chest.

He toppled and fell as she threw herself at him. She scrabbled for the rug, throwing it over him, trying to roll the heavy body, seeing all the time his horror-filled eyes and blistering skin.

The flames died inside the rug. Jonny was whimpering, like a beaten dog, mental pain still drowning the physical pain of the burns.

As she dialled 999, the numbing effect of the drink or drugs gave way. Jonny's agonised screams were worse than the stench of burnt flesh.

CHAPTER SIXTEEN

'Jesus, Mary and Joseph.'

Bill Wilson was not a man given to cursing. Rhona took the stiff whisky he handed her. She shook so much she had to guide the glass to her mouth using both hands.

'Jonny wanted to tell me something. I'm sure of it.' Rhona felt the whisky slide down her throat, warming her. She sat the glass on the coffee table and clasped her hands to steady them.

'Maybe he was about to confess.'

She shook her head. 'I don't think so. I went to *Eden* tonight.'

'What?' Bill's voice was incredulous.

'Belcher didn't recognise me. I made sure of that. He was too interested in important guests anyway.'

'You think Jonny followed you from there?'

She gave a brief nod. 'I got into Belcher's office.'

There was a sharp intake of breath.

She rushed on before he could protest. 'There's a screen behind a painting. Belcher watches all the private rooms from there.'

Bill thought about that. 'He saw Donna's rose man.'

'He must have.'

Bill's mouth was tight with anger. 'I'll have him for obstructing our enquiries.'

'There were three men there for a private showing,' she went on. 'I think I recognised one of them. Something to do with football. I saw him leave and took a note of the number plate.'

She handed him the scribbled number.

'If Belcher's covering for someone,' Bill threatened.

'My bet is he's covering for most of his clientele. The ones with money at least.'

'But would he cover a murder?'

Rhona gave him a look. 'Maybe.'

Bill raised his eyebrows. 'Okay. What else?'

'I found an inhaler in the desk drawer in

Belcher's office.'

That threw him. 'So he could have been close to Donna before she died?'

'If the inhaler is his.'

When Bill left, Rhona poured another whisky and crawled into bed. She recognised she was in shock, but couldn't stop the trembling. She sat upright, the duvet hugged round her. When her mobile rang, she could hardly pick it up for shaking.

'Rhona. It's me. I know it's really late but I need to see you.'

'I..I..don..don't know.'

'Rhona? Are you okay?'

'Sean... ' her voice faded.

'I'll be right over.'

'No!'

'But...'

She didn't want sympathy. It would make her feel worse. Her voice was stronger now. 'I can't explain right now, but I don't want you to come.'

There was a moment's silence.

'I'll call you tomorrow,' she offered.

'Sure.' His voice was cool.

She suspected Sean was not used to being turned down.

When he rang off she fetched another duvet from the spare room. Wrapped in one, she lay with the other over her. The cat jumped up and wriggled in underneath. Rhona lay, eyes open, shivering, remembering only flames and Jonny's terrified eyes.

CHAPTER SEVENTEEN

After he left Rhona's flat Bill headed for the hospital. He called Jonny's mate, Alistair Banks, on the way there.

Banks appeared half an hour later, looking pretty shaken up. When they wouldn't let him see Jonny that shook him up even more. Sitting in the corridor with Bill, he revealed that Jonny hadn't shown up for his shift the night Donna died. Alistair had covered for him.

'Why didn't you say anything about this before?'

'He was screwed up. I didn't want to make things worse.'

Bill had difficulty holding himself back as he waited for Banks to go on.

'Jonny thought Donna was seeing some guy from her days at the club. I tried to tell him it was rubbish.'

'And he didn't believe you?'

'No. He was pretty mad.'

'At Donna?'

Banks spoke as though he was trying to convince himself. 'Jonny was hard on Donna sometimes, but he would never hurt her.'

'What if he was sure Donna was sleeping with someone else?'

Banks looked stupidly at Bill. 'What?'

'The landlord says another man – not Jonny – visited Donna in her room the night before she died. He stayed a long time.'

'Fuck!' Banks' world was crashing round him.

'If Jonny knew about that, would it be enough for him to kill Donna?'

Banks didn't answer, but Bill saw the shadow of doubt in his eyes. He ran the scenario over in his own mind, just the way Banks was doing.

Jonny suspected Donna was playing away. When he found out his suspicions were correct, he killed her in a fit of jealousy and rage. Then he realised Tracey suspected him. So she had to go too. But drink couldn't blot out what he'd done. So he set fire to himself.

Bill took Banks to the police station and got a statement, then he asked him for a DNA sample. Banks agreed but didn't look happy about it.

'We'll be sampling everyone at the fire station,' Bill told him.

They needed to find this other guy. If Banks couldn't tell them who he was, maybe Belcher could.

Next day Bill sent DC Clarke and a colleague to question the other members of Jonny's watch and collect DNA samples. He wanted to know exactly who was on the outing when Jonny first met Donna. He suspected that hadn't been the only time men from the fire station had visited *Eden*. He wanted everything. Names, dates and who had danced for them. Tracey had said the guy who visited Donna regularly was young and worked out, which meant he could have been a fireman.

Bill delayed his own arrival at *Eden* with his search warrant until the club was open and packed with lunchtime punters. All the better to watch Belcher shit himself.

He ordered a police presence on all doors and gave orders to his Detective Sergeant.

'No one is allowed to leave the premises until their contact details are recorded and a DNA swab is taken.'

Belcher's face was wearing enough sweat to fry chips. Bill flashed the search warrant and demanded to be taken to the manager's office.

The fat man's breath was a painful wheeze as he unlocked the office door. It got worse when Bill headed straight for the painting and pulled it back to reveal the hidden screen.

Bill opened the top drawer of the desk and took out the inhaler.

'I think you need some of this.'

CHAPTER EIGHTEEN

Rhona was surviving... just. Chrissy had offered to listen if she needed an ear. Rhona said no. Talking made it too real. The news from the hospital wasn't good. Jonny was badly burned around the upper torso including his face. He wouldn't be fit to talk for a while.

Belcher's arrest and grilling by DI Wilson had produced a client list so short the club must be making a loss. The search of the premises was more productive. They found a hidden store of tapes, secretly recorded by Belcher. According to him they were for his eyes only. Watching the girls perform was his way of having sex. He insisted they knew about it and he paid them extra to do it. And yes he needed to use his inhaler when he got excited. He couldn't or wouldn't say why Donna's hair had traces of salbutomal.

A police team was going through the video footage. Especially footage of the Rose room. If there was evidence that *Eden* was being used for prostitution, Belcher was in big trouble.

The best lead they had was the car number plate. It belonged to a Sir Geoffrey Helden who was bankrolling a Scottish first division football club. DI Wilson had already made contact and would speak to Sir Geoffrey with his lawyer present.

Rhona spent the morning putting the Bacardi bottle back together. Concentrating on that stopped her thinking about what had happened the night before. When the phone rang, Rhona let Chrissy answer.

Chrissy covered the mouthpiece. 'There's a guy in reception. Insists on seeing you.'

'Who?' Rhona mouthed.

Chrissy checked. 'Sean?'

Rhona shook her head and then thought better of it. She would have to face Sean sometime and it might as well be now.

'Tell him I'll be straight down.'

It was the first time she'd seen Sean agitated.

Normally he was relaxed and easy. When she appeared he looked over, relieved.

She headed for the door without speaking and he followed. She walked quickly past the guard on the gate and down the hill towards the park, her breath condensing in the cold November air. When she reached the bridge she stopped. Below, an autumnal mist clung to the River Kelvin.

He stood close, sharing her view of the muddy swirling water.

'What's wrong?'

She shrugged, unable to look him in the face. 'It's nothing to do with you. It's work.'

He lifted his hand and stroked her cheek. A shiver of longing ran down her spine and anchored itself deep in her groin.

'You can't work all the time.'

She laughed. The sound was harsh and unforgiving in her ears.

'Rhona. Look at me.'

His eyes drew hers. Powerless to stop herself, she looked into their blue depths. She hardly knew this man and yet she had let him enter her body, possess her, at least for a short time. What was he really like? How much of herself could she entrust to him?

'Tell me when I can see you.'

'Tonight.' She gave in to desire. 'Come round tonight.'

His finger traced her cheek, her lips, her neck. He didn't kiss her, though he knew she wanted him to.

She watched as he headed for the Art Gallery; the tall dark-haired figure confident now. She felt like a tune Sean had chosen to play.

CHAPTER NINETEEN

Donna and Jonny's text messages were designed for their eyes only. Three quarters of them were short, repetitive and sexual. A sex act by phone. Bill imagined Jonny sitting in the long night shift, putting in time by fantasising.

The tone only changed near Donna's death. Tense and angry, Jonny demanded to know where Donna was and why she didn't answer. Jonny was running scared. Scared and jealous.

They had never recovered Donna's mobile. Bill was beginning to think Tracey had removed it from the handbag before they arrived at the scene of Donna's death. If Tracey listened to the messages, did that make her suspicious of someone? Is that why she was killed?

He'd insisted on interviewing every footballer who used the lap dancing club, which hadn't gone down well with the Superintendent. Bill didn't care.

He didn't like any of them on principle. Beckham look-a-likes with money and an inflated sense of their own importance.

The one that sat in front of him now was different. Quietly spoken. Slightly built with the intensity of a young Jimmy Johnstone.

Thomas Watkins. Bill had seen the name in the paper a lot recently. A rising star. Scotland's hope for the future. A lot of pressure for a nineteen year old.

Bill pushed Donna's photo across the interview table.

'Donna Stevens. Known to you as Rose.'

Thomas gave the photo a quick glance. Too quick.

'Sorry. Don't know her.'

Bill consulted his notebook. 'You and three mates booked Rose on the night of the... '

'We booked Rose, but it wasn't this girl.'

Bill withdrew Donna's picture and substituted Tracey's battered body.

The face went white. Bill could swear he heard the stomach churn.

Watkins' voice was a whisper. 'That's her.'

Bill waited.

Watkins cleared his throat. 'My mates were a bit high. She chose me first, probably because I wasn't as drunk as them. I liked her but the rest of the guys gave her a hard time.'

'How?'

'Called her names, handled her... ' He wasn't proud of this.

'And?'

'I went back to apologise the next day. We drank champagne. She danced. I left.'

'You brought your own rose.'

He looked startled. 'How did you know...'

'You bought roses in Marks and Spencers. Someone recognised you.'

'I bought a bunch. I was going to give them to her to apologise.'

'And then you poisoned her.'

'What?'

'Tracey was given strychnine in a drink.'

'Not by me.'

'Then dumped in a skip.'

'No!'

He was shocked, but there was fear there too.

Fear that he was linked in some way to the crime. Bill went for it.

'The mouth swab you gave. What if I told you we found a DNA match in Donna's flat.'

Watkins thought about that. 'You can't have. You're lying.'

Bill was, but he didn't let it show. 'Amazing what you find between the sheets – bits of skin, hair, semen. I believe you had sex with Donna Stevens the night she died.'

For a moment, Bill thought his instinct was wrong. Then Watkins' face crumpled: 'Okay. Okay. I was with her that night. But I didn't kill her.'

Bill waited patiently.

'She really wanted that dress. Showed me a picture of it. She said her boyfriend would kill her if he found out...' he stopped suddenly realising what he'd said.

'Go on.'

'That was supposed to be the last time I saw her. One last time, that's what she said.'

'But you didn't want that, did you?'

A quick flush crept up the pale neck and across the face.

'You were angry with Donna because she wouldn't see you again. And you'd spent all that money on her.'

Watkins swallowed hard, his lips trembling. Bill almost felt sorry for him.

'I want to speak to my solicitor.'

'I think you'd better.'

CHAPTER TWENTY

There were hardly any bits missing, only slithers here and there. If you looked at it casually, you were looking at a whole bottle.

Rhona dusted it all over with lampblack powder, pulled over the light and lifted the magnifying glass. Donna was the last person to handle the bottle, most likely by the neck. But Donna had been wearing long black gloves as part of her devil's outfit.

Rhona concentrated the magnifying glass on the lower part of the bottle. When she spotted the print, her heart leapt in her chest. She quickly took a series of photos. Then applied the lifting tape.

Her old mentor had been right. A murderer will always leave something of himself at the scene of crime, however well hidden.

'I have a print from the broken bottle.'

Bill was incredulous. 'How the hell did you do that?'

'I'll explain later. I ran a check on it and a name came up. Alec Bankfoot. Convicted of assault on a prostitute in 1995, sentenced to two years.'

'But Thomas Watkins was the one with the rose.'

'Watkins didn't kill Donna or Tracey.'

'But we thought Donna knew her killer.'

'She did.' A horrible thought had entered her head. 'Is there a policeman guarding Jonny Simpson?'

'No. But his mate Banks has taken time off work to sit with him. Seems he's there round the clock.'

There was a brief silence as they both digested this. Then Rhona said:

'I'll meet you at the hospital in fifteen minutes.'

The room smelt of disinfectant and singed flesh. Jonny lay still and alone. Rhona pulled up a chair and sat beside him. She tried to imagine what it would be like to lose your love in such a way and to feel responsible.

She would probably want to die. It would be the only way to truly forget.

Banks came in and stood behind her.

'How is he?' she said.

'He's going to die.'

'They've told you that?'

'He's given up. I'm his mate. I can feel it.'

She looked up at his cold furious face.

'That bitch did this. I told him what she was, but he wouldn't listen. He wanted to marry her, can you believe it? You screw bitches like that, you don't marry them.'

He turned away. 'I'm going for a coffee.'

She waited until he was at the door before she called him back.

'Alec!'

He turned instinctively. For a moment he didn't know what he'd done. Then realisation dawned on his face and he came at her.

She tried to duck the blow but he was too quick, a fireman's reaction. His big hand circled her neck. She felt herself lift off the floor then the lights went out.

Somewhere in the darkness she heard Bill's voice shout her name.

CHAPTER TWENTY-ONE

'Banks was seeing Donna before Jonny met her at the club. He was obsessed by her. When Jonny started to go out with Donna, Banks did everything he could to stop it. To him Donna was a thing. To Jonny she was the woman he loved. Donna didn't tell Jonny about Banks. Firemen are close mates. They have to be. Their lives depend on it. Sharing women screws that up. But she told Tracey. Which is why Tracey died.'

'Donna loved Jonny,' Rhona said.

'That's what Banks hated most. The fact they loved each other. Donna used what she had to give herself a future.'

'A fairytale wedding dress.'

'A romantic trying to live in the real world,' Bill said.

Rhona smiled. 'A bit like yourself.'

'So. What's happening with the saxophone player?'

'How do I explain fingerprint bruising on my neck?'

'You'll think of something.'

Sean fell asleep as soon as they finishing making love. The French called such sudden sleep, *the little death*. Rhona reached out and touched the warm cheek.

Love and death.

When she explained about the bruising on her neck, Sean had called her Lady Death. At the height of passion it sounded sexy and exciting.

When he woke, Rhona was in the kitchen making coffee. Sean wrapped his arms about her and placed a kiss in the hollow of her neck.

'What you said... about us... ' she began.

He turned her round, hope on his face.

'Yes?'

'We could give it a try?'

Rhona remembered the scent of Sean's skin long after he left. She walked through the flat, imagining him there, wondering how it would feel to share her space with him... and found herself smiling.

She and Sean were bound together now. For how long, she had no way of knowing.

Published with this volume

GATO
Margaret Elphinstone

An unusual love story set in the Middle Ages, Gato is the story of a young child brought up in a mill. The quiet hardworking lives of the people at the mill are disturbed by the arrival of a wandering Spanish Friar. What is going on between the miller and his wife, and the Friar? The child at the centre of the story tries to understand. The only creatures the child is close to are the mill cats. After the Friar's stay, there is always one called Gato, Spanish for 'cat'.

Margaret Elphinstone has written six other novels, four of which are historical. She began writing in Shetland in the 1970s. As well as being a writer she has worked as a gardener, library assistant, home help and lecturer. She now lives in Glasgow and is Professor of Writing at the University of Strathclyde. She has two daughters.

THESE TIMES, THIS PLACE
Muriel Gray

Edited by Moira Forsyth

We need good writers to tackle hard topics.
Maternity pay, public transport, gap year students,
poor housing – things that matter to us all. Muriel
Gray tells us why they do, and what needs to be
done. You might agree with her or you might not –
but you certainly won't be bored when you
read these articles from her regular
Sunday Herald column.

Muriel Gray began her media career in 1982
with Channel 4's music show *The Tube*. She went on
to present programmes such as *Frocks on the Box*, a
long running fashion series, and *Bliss*, a teenage
music and culture show. She has also presented
many Edinburgh Festival programmes, as well
as the *The Media Show* on Channel 4. She began
her own production company in 1987, now
part of IWC Media.

The first woman rector of Edinburgh University,
Muriel Gray is also a best selling author, with *The
First Fifty*, (a book about the Munro Mountains)
and three horror novels.

She lives in Glasgow with her husband and three
children. After her family, her other passions are
mountaineering, snowboarding and growing trees.

Also available

THE CHERRY SUNDAE COMPANY
Isla Dewar

THE BLUE HEN
Des Dillon

THE WHITE CLIFFS
Suhayl Saadi

Moira Forsyth, *Series Editor for the Sandstone Vistas, writes:*

The Sandstone Vista Series of books has been developed for readers who are not used to reading full length novels, or for those who simply want to enjoy a 'quick read' which is satisfying and well written.